A Storyteller Book

Cinderella

by Charles Perrault

Retold by Lesley Young
Illustrated by Annabel Spenceley

ARMADILLO

There was once a beautiful girl with golden hair and eyes as blue as the sky. She was very happy, until her mother became ill and died. Her father married again, but soon he died, too, and she was left with her stepmother and her two stepsisters.

They were very ugly, bad-tempered girls, and they were so jealous of her beauty that they made her wear an old dress and wooden shoes.

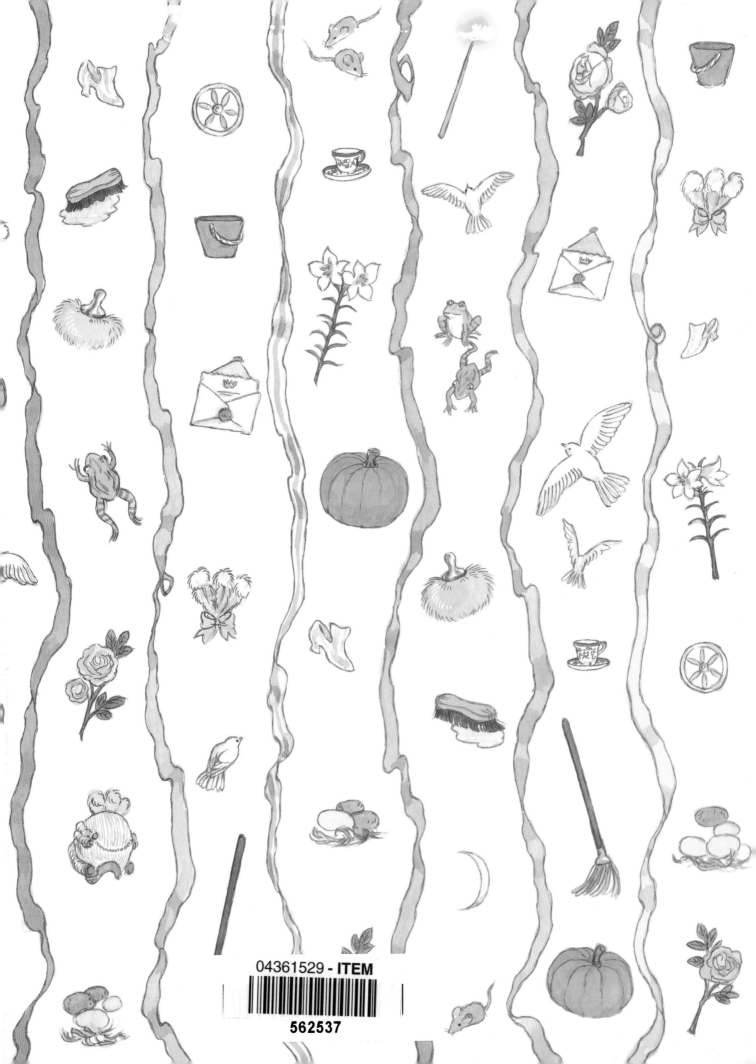

This edition is published by Armadillo,
an imprint of Anness Publishing Ltd, Blaby Road,
Wigston, Leicestershire LE18 4SE; info@anness.com

www.annesspublishing.com

If you like the images in this book and would like to investigate using
them for publishing, promotions or advertising, please visit our website
www.practicalpictures.com for more information.

A CIP catalogue record for this book is available from the British Library.

Publisher: Joanna Lorenz
Editorial Consultant: Jackie Fortey
Project Editor: Richard McGinlay
Designer: Sarah Hodder
Production Controller: Steve Lang

PUBLISHER'S NOTE
The author and publishers have made every effort to ensure that this book
is safe for its intended use, and cannot accept any legal responsibility
or liability for any harm or injury arising from misuse.

Manufacturer: Anness Publishing Ltd,
Blaby Road, Wigston, Leicestershire LE18 4SE, England
For Product Tracking go to: www.annesspublishing.com/tracking
Batch: 1015-22581-1127

"It's your job to scrub the house, clean out the fire and cook," they told her.

She had to get up very early to fetch water from the well, and she spent all day on her hands and knees scrubbing, or making the meals.

"Ugh! We don't like this stew! It's disgusting!" shouted her stepsisters, as they gobbled down the meals she made.

No matter what she did, it was never good enough.

"Have you turned my mattress? There's a lump in it," said one. "Go and do it now!"

"That's nothing!" said the other, "I just found a feather in my pigeon pie!"

They made their stepsister wash and iron their fine dresses and the ribbons in their hair. But even in her old tatty dress, her eyes shone out like the blue sky and she made her stepsisters look uglier than ever.

At the end of a hard day, the girl had no warm bath to soak in or soft bed to sleep in. The poor girl used to huddle down beside the warm cinders of the fire, so she became known as Cinderella.

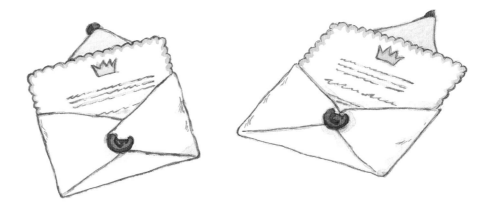

One morning, Cinderella carried through a steaming pile of toast, trying hard not to drop it. The two stepsisters were sitting at the table waving large white cards with gold crowns on them, and they were pink with excitement.

"There's a Grand Ball at the palace – and we're invited."

"The King has decided it's time for his son, the Prince, to choose a bride," said their mother. "He's asked all the girls in the land to the ball, so that he may choose one to be his wife."

"Am I invited then?" asked Cinderella.

"You?" screeched her stepmother, "in your rags, with smuts on your face?" and they all laughed so much that Cinderella rushed back to the kitchen and sobbed beside the fire.

Soon the night of the ball came.

"Pull tighter!" said her stepsisters, as Cinderella laced them into their silk ball gowns. She curled their hair with iron tongs, heated in the fire.

"Don't burn it!" they cried, "You're not making pastry now!" At last they were painted and powdered and covered in perfume. Cinderella couldn't help sneezing.

"Stop that!" they shouted. "You're only sneezing because you're jealous. Go and see if our carriage is there yet, and make us a snack for the journey."

Their mother appeared wearing bright blue silk, with feathers in her hair, looking like a plump, red-faced peacock. Then they all swept off in their carriage and, after all the hurry and fuss, Cinderella was quite alone.

She cleared up the powder and perfume and went back to the kitchen, but she was too sad to eat her scraps of bread and cheese. She opened the door and threw the bread out for the birds, as she did every night.

There was already a pale, watery moon in the sky. As she stood looking up at it, Cinderella wished with all her heart that she, too, could go to the ball.

Cinderella went back inside and sat down beside the kitchen fire and, as she thought about the grand ballroom and the handsome prince, a tear fell and sizzled on the grate.

"Why are you crying?" asked a gentle voice behind her. "And what are you doing here when you should be at the ball?"

Cinderella looked round and blinked. A little old lady in a red cloak stood there, with a round smiling face and a wand which sparkled at the tip like a firefly.

"How can I go to the ball," said Cinderella, "in these rags? How can I dance in these heavy wooden shoes? You don't know how much I long to dance!"

"Oh yes I do," said the old lady. "I am your fairy godmother," and she tapped Cinderella on the shoulder with the wand. At once Cinderella's rags vanished, and she was wearing a white silk ball gown that glittered with diamonds.

She twirled round and the silk swished and rustled, leaving a trail of perfume that was so gentle that it almost wasn't there. It smelled like summer rain.

Cinderella's feet felt as light as air, and when she looked down she saw beautiful glass slippers, twinkling in the firelight.

"Now you will go to the ball," said the fairy godmother.

"But there is no carriage to take me," said Cinderella.

The old lady looked round the kitchen. She picked up an apple and looked at it carefully. "No . . . Wait a minute, do you see that big pumpkin?" she said, pointing to the vegetable basket. "Help me carry it out into the garden."

She tapped it with her wand and, as Cinderella stared, it changed before her eyes into a glass coach that sparkled like ice. But what use was a glass coach with no horses?

Six fieldmice crouched nearby, dazzled by the shiny coach. The old lady tapped them lightly on their ears. They disappeared and in their place stood six white horses, tossing their manes in the night air.

"You need footmen – one to drive, and one to ride behind and make sure you arrive safely," said the old lady. She lifted a large leaf with her wand, and two frogs peeped out. When she tapped them with the wand, they vanished to be replaced by two footmen with white wigs and bulging eyes.

"Look after your mistress," she said.

"We will," they croaked.

"Now, off you go the the ball, "said the fairy godmother. "But listen carefully and don't ever forget this – you must leave the palace before midnight. At the last stroke of Twelve, all your fine clothes will disappear and you will be back in your old tatty rags." Cinderella promised, and thanked her with tears in her eyes, as she climbed into the coach.

"Oh, thank you again!" she shouted through the window, as the glass coach swept off in a cloud of dust.

At the palace, the ballroom blazed with the light from hundreds of candles. When Cinderella appeared at the top of the staircase, everyone stopped dancing and stared at her, wondering who the beautiful young stranger was. The band stopped playing and the Prince looked round to see what was happening.

"I think she must be a foreign princess," sniffed one of her stepsisters, never dreaming that this was Cinderella.

The Prince at once ran up the stairs, took her hands in his, and asked her to dance. As the music struck up again, and she was swept off in his arms, Cinderella felt that all her dreams had come true.

She had never learned to dance, but the glass slippers seemed to make it very easy and she felt as if she was floating on air. All evening, the Prince danced only with her. When others came up to ask her to dance, he held her hands tightly in his own and said, "No. This is my partner."

The Prince took her in to supper, and she ate a water ice that tasted like violets. At another table, she could see her stepsisters quarrelling over the last cherry in a bowl of ice cream. As she watched, her stepmother reached over and ate it herself. But Cinderella was too excited to eat much.

The Prince led her off again into the music. As they danced, he leaned down and said, "Did you know that your eyes are just like the sky?"

When he whispered in her ear, "Will you be my princess?"
Cinderella felt she could dance with him for ever. But then she
was startled by a loud noise like a gong.

"What's that?"

"Don't worry," laughed the Prince, "it's only the palace clock
striking midnight, although it seems only seconds since we met."

"Midnight!" cried Cinderella, and she broke away from him
and rushed out of the ballroom.

The guests drew back on either side to let her through, and the Prince ran after her, but she raced like the wind down the steps.

"Quick!" shouted the Prince. "Find her!"

Footmen ran off in all directions, looking for her, but she had vanished into the night.

In fact, Cinderella had climbed into the palace dovecot to hide. The doves knew that she was kind and fed birds in the cold weather, and they didn't make a noise. They sat at the entrance, spreading their feathers and hiding Cinderella, and the footmen ran past and never thought to look inside.

At last Cinderella was able to climb down and run home, wearing her old dress again.

But back at the palace, the Prince was holding something that sparkled in the moonlight. Cinderella had been in such a hurry that one of her glass slippers had fallen off and been left behind on the palace steps.

The Prince held it up. "I have found my princess, "he said." She is the owner of this slipper."

When her stepmother arrived back from the ball with her stepsisters, Cinderella was sitting in her old tatty dress at her usual place beside the fire.

"Quick! Undo our laces!" screeched the sisters, throwing themselves into chairs and easing off their shoes to rub their feet.

"Bring me some tea!" said her stepmother, taking pins out of her hair. "So many people wanted to dance with us, we didn't have time to eat. What a ball! Isn't it a shame you'll never see such a thing? You can't imagine the dresses. And the jewels!"

"Isn't the Prince wonderful to dance with?" said one of the sisters.

"Oh, divine!" said the other, winking.

"And there was a mysterious foreign princess," said their mother, pouring her tea into her saucer. "It's so exciting – just like a fairy tale."

The Prince carried the glass slipper with him everywhere. He couldn't sleep, and said he would not rest until he had found his princess again. Then he had an idea and he sent for two of his best footmen.

"I want you to take this slipper and travel all over the land," he told them, "making sure that every girl in the country tries it on. I don't want to see you again until you have found the girl whose foot it fits."

For six days the footmen rushed all over the country, to grand houses, farms and cottages.

Every girl tried to make the slipper fit her. The girl in the dairy stopped churning butter and rubbed some on her foot, to try and make it slip inside. Grand ladies soaked their feet in hot perfumed water to see if they would shrink.

On the seventh day, the footmen arrived at Cinderella's house. Her stepsisters rushed to try on the glass slipper.

"I wondered where I'd lost that!" said one.

"Don't be silly, you know it's mine," said the other.

They huffed and puffed and screwed up their toes, but it was no use. They couldn't jam their feet into the dainty slipper.

"Is there no one else in the house?" asked the footmen.

"Only Cinderella," snorted the stepmother. "But she's just a servant, and she certainly doesn't go to balls."

"The Prince said that every girl must try it on," said the footmen. "Let her try."

The sisters went into the kitchen, where Cinderella was peeling a huge mound of potatoes.

"You're wanted in the drawing-room," they said, "but don't bother to wash, you'll be back peeling potatoes in a minute."

Cinderella went through, and a footman held out the glass slipper. She slipped her foot into it, and it fitted as if it had been made for her. Behind her, the ugly sisters gasped as she reached into a pocket in her old dress and pulled out the other glass slipper. It matched perfectly.

"There must be some mistake," spluttered her stepmother.

"There is no mistake," said the footmen. "This is our new princess – look how beautiful she is, with eyes like the sky." They took off their hats and bowed in front of Cinderella.

"We have a gold coach outside," said one. "Will you come with us now to the palace?"

Cinderella was still holding the potato knife. She handed it to one of her stepsisters, who took it as if it were a rose, and curtseyed.

"Can we come, too?" they squealed, "We are her sisters."

The footmen placed a cloak of sky blue silk over Cinderella's shoulders and said, "Hurry. The Prince is waiting."

The stepsisters and their mother were left in the courtyard, their mouths hanging open, as Cinderella went off in her golden coach.

The Prince stood at the top of the Palace steps and held out his arms in welcome. Cinderella ran up the steps, and the doves flew beside her, holding up her cloak.

"At last I have found my Princess," said the Prince, holding her to him, "and I'm never going to let you go this time."

More invitations were sent out, this time to a royal wedding.

In Cinderella's old home, her stepsisters had to make their own breakfast. "How can I make toast when you've let the fire go out?" snapped one.

"Oh, do it yourself," said the other. "It's all your fault. If we'd been nicer to Cinderella, we would have been asked to the wedding."

But then there was a knock at the door, and there stood a footman with a stiff white envelope. The stepsisters tore it open and found invitations to the royal wedding inside. Cinderella was so happy that she couldn't bear the thought of anyone being unhappy – even the stepsisters who had been so unkind to her.

The palace cook made twenty different kinds of
ice cream, and baked a cake that was big enough
for everyone in the country to have a slice.

On the morning of the wedding, the ballroom
was filled with so many white lilies and rose
trees, that it looked like a garden.

At the wedding party, the Prince held Cinderella tightly and said, "You're not going to disappear at midnight again, are you?"

"Never," replied Cinderella, and she went to the top of the staircase and looked through the crowd until she spotted her stepsisters, clinging to each other sadly in a corner.

Then she took her wedding bouquet of white roses and threw it down at them. They stretched up, caught it, and for a moment they didn't look ugly at all.

Turning back to the Prince, Cinderella smiled and said, "Wouldn't it be lovely if everyone could live happily ever after – just like us?"

The End

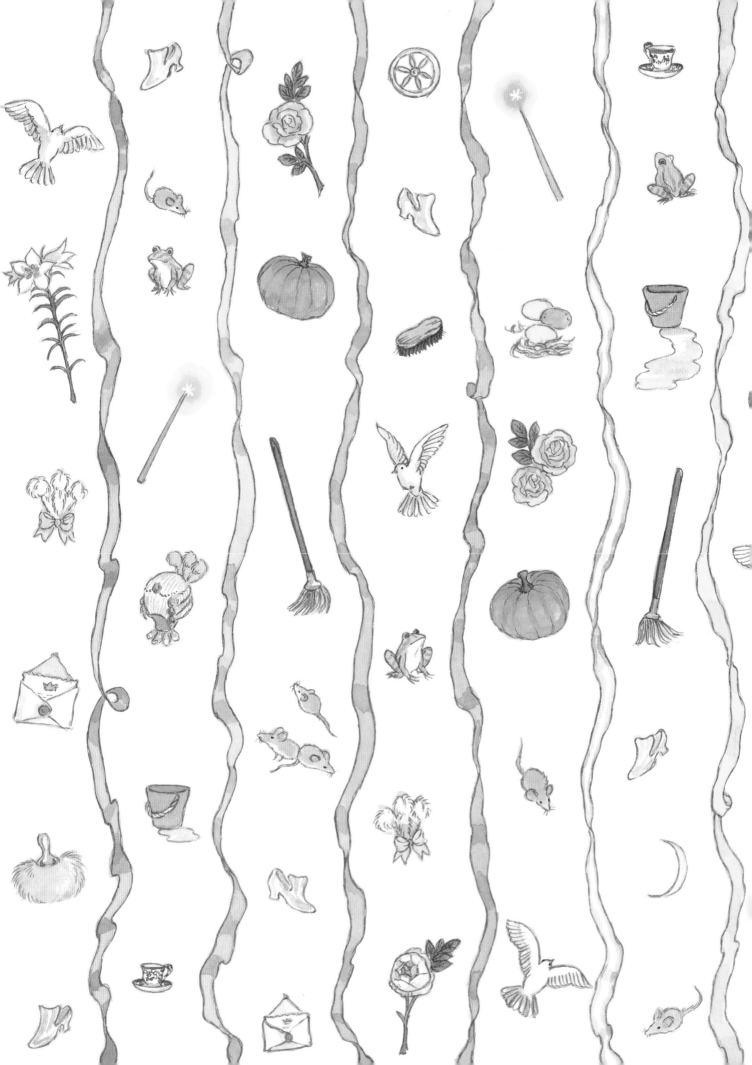

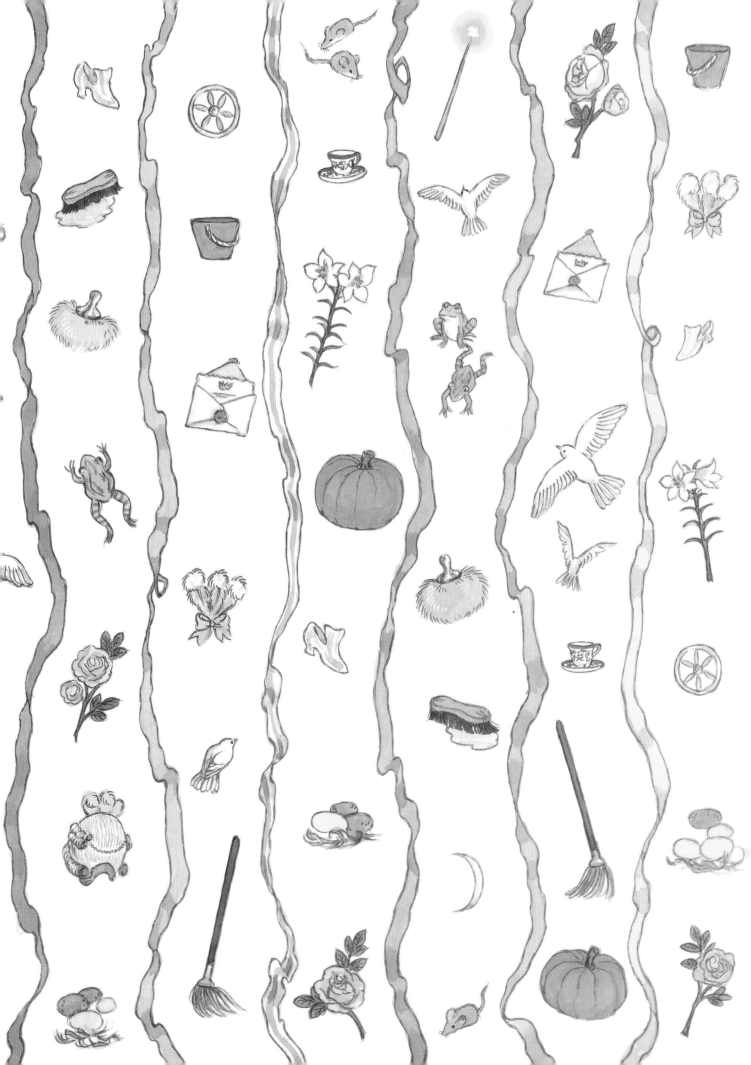